LEONORA CARRINGTON

The Milk of Dreams

THE NEW YORK REVIEW CHILDREN'S COLLECTION

New York

THIS IS A NEW YORK REVIEW BOOK
PUBLISHED BY THE NEW YORK REVIEW OF BOOKS
435 Hudson Street, New York, NY 10014
www.nyrb.com

Published in Spanish is *Leche del sueño*.

A catalog record for this book is available from the Library of Congress

ISBN 978-1-68137-094-1
Available as an electronic book; ISBN 978-1-68137-095-8

Design by Katy Homans

Printed in the United States of America on acid-free paper.

4 6 8 0 9 7 6 5 3

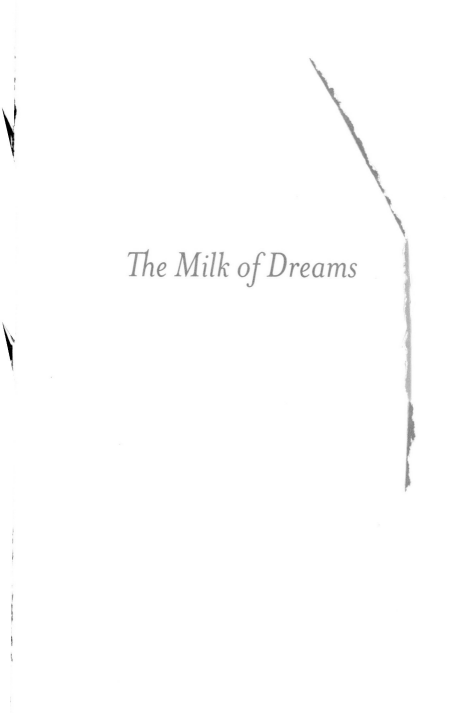

The Milk of Dreams

Headless John

The boy had wings instead of ears.

He looked strange.

"Look at my ears," he said.
The people were afraid.

During the night John liked moving his ears.
One night he moved them so much that his
    head flew out of the window.
With no head he couldn't even cry.

SO

He got up and he ran after his head, which
was flying from tree to tree as if it were a
pigeon.

John's mama, who was looking out of the
window, saw her child running around at
night.

"Where are you going?"

"My head took off."

"What a pity," said the poor woman.

"Ha. Ha. Ha. That's right," laughed the head.

John ran very fast but he could not catch his
     head. He kept flying along, laughing.

"Lend me a string," said John to a man.

"Here, take it," he said.

John caught his head and went home very
    tired with the head jumping along behind
    him firmly tied to the string.

"Mama," he said, "stick on my head please,"
   and his Mama stuck on his head with
   chewing gum, but because it was night
   time she stuck it on backwards.
"Don't let your head escape again," she said,
   and from there on John was very careful.

The Child George

George liked eating the wall of his room.
"Don't do it," said his father.
George went on eating wall.

His father went to the
Drug Store and bought
a bottle of wall pills.

George ate
them all and
his head grew
into a house.

George was happy playing with the house, but
the father was sad because everybody said:
"What a strange child you have, Sir."

Humbert the Beautiful

Humbert was the most beautiful boy in the town.

He had blue eyes and golden curls.

He was very beautiful, but he was nasty.

He liked putting rats in the beds of his sisters.

The little girls cried.

One day Rose, his sister, put a crocodile in
his bed.

"AI," yelled Humbert, "I'm afraid there's a
crocodile in my bed!"

But Humbert was so beautiful the crocodile gave
him an agreeable smile. Humbert and the
crocodile had become friends.

The child is even nastier than he was before
because he goes everywhere with the
crocodile.

The Monster of Chihuahua

When the moon is thin the monster walks
   this street.
It was called Chavela Ortiz.
It had no residence.
No husband.
No mother.
No father.
No children.
BUT
It had six legs, a golden jewel and pearls,
   and there it kept the portrait of Don
   Angel Vidrio Gonzalez, the head of the
   Sanitary Department.
The monster said: "Fives and fours, fives and
   fours, fives and fours, 5+4, 5+4, 5+4,"
   and after that the monster made up the
   total.

Here is Señorita Gomez Castillo sewing pyjamas for her child.

This appears to be a monkey.

But this is a monkey in a forest with water.

Señor Mustache Mustache who has two faces—
eats flies, dances—here is his turkey.

And here is his little girl who eats spiders—
she's sick.

In addition,
Señora Mustache
Mustache upside
down. They are
all very ugly.

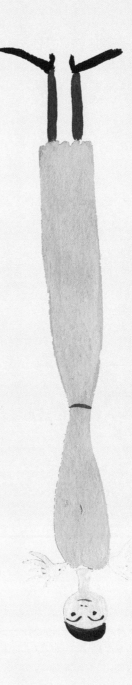

The bunny's
pretty, but it's
not theirs.

This boy smoked a
cigarette—his Papa let
him have it.

The boy cried—his Papa
kissed him.

Then they went to the
movies. The boy doesn't
smoke anymore.

Two birds.

They're going to the movies too.

This one is not going,
because he has already
seen the movie.

The Horrible Story of the Little Meats

Mrs. Dolores Catapum de la Garza was old, ugly, a nasty person, and smelled of caca.

This woman was so ugly that her friends called her Lolita Stomach.

Lolita had a taco stall in the market. Lolita always had a little box of rotten meat which she gave to children and then they had a stomach ache.

She didn't like children at all.

One morning very early Lolita saw three children talking to each other.

"Let's go to the woods and find little herbs and humming bird's eggs," said the boy.

He was the biggest. His name was Vincent.
"Yes, let's go," said Tomasina, and the
   smallest jumped up and down with joy.
The three children went happily off to the
   woods.

BUT

Lolita went after them with her little box of
rotten meat.

The children were playing in the woods when
Lolita arrived.

"Little children," she said with a horrible
smile, "come and eat some meat, it's
really very good."

Lolita put out her black tongue and the
children were afraid.

When she opened the box the little meats
jumped out on their own they were so
rotten.

"We'd better not eat them," said Vincent,
"because then we'll have a stomach ache."

"Just you eat them up," said Lolita, and she
left the little meats on the ground and
they were running here and there like
mice. They smelled terrible.

"Foutchi," said Tomasina, pinching her nose.

Shortly afterwards Lolita came back.

"Did you eat the little meats?" she asked.

"Yes, yes," said the children.

"Little lies," said Lolita.

"Oh yes, we ate the little meats," said the
children.

"All right," said Lolita, "those little meats
could not only run around but they could
also talk."

So the ugly old woman called the little meats
and asked them: "Have any of you been
eaten by these children?"

"No, No," shouted all the little meats in
chorus, "they didn't eat anything, not even
half."

So Lolita caught hold of the three children.

"All right, you're ungrateful. I'm going to
cut you up in little pieces."

The children cried a lot.

She took them away and
she cut off their heads.

She put them in a big cage.

The parrot didn't live
there any more.

Lolita was pleased.

"These children have
   no heads," she said,
   and she hung up
   the heads in her
   wardrobe.
BUT
The Green Indian
   arrived and opened
   Lolita's wardrobe.
   He wanted to steal
   her shawl.
He saw the three
   heads of the
   children crying.
"Poor little ones," said the Green Indian.
   "Where are your bodies?"
"They're in the parrot's cage," said Vincent.
So the Green Indian stuck on their heads
   again.
However, the Green Indian was stupid and
   he didn't know where to stick them.
Tomasina had her head stuck to her hand.

The little one had it stuck under his foot, and
    Vincent had his stuck on his behind.
Poor Vincent, every time he sat down his
    face shouted "AI."
"They look all right," said the Green Indian.
    He was stupid.
The children went home.
"What happened?" said their father.

But the children were
    happy in spite of
    having their heads
    stuck on such funny
    places.

The Nasty Story of the Camomile Tea

Little Angel was sick.

He had Flu.

His mama shut him up in his room.

"Little Angel, don't get out of your bed," said his mama.

"Oh no, mama," said Little Angel.

She had hardly gone out when Little Angel jumped out of bed and opened the window.

A lady was passing by underneath.

Little Angel made pipi over her.

The lady said: "It's raining,"
    and she started to run.

Little Angel liked this.

Little Angel took some
    more Camomile Tea
    so he could make some
    more pipi.

A gentleman passed and
    Little Angel made pipi
    again.

The gentleman's hat was all
    wet with pipi.

"I'll hit you," he yelled, very
        angry.

Little Angel hid himself.

        The gentleman went away
            shouting: "Those
            people are pigs."

33

Little Angel stayed in bed until the elephant
    and the horse came in.
They both made pipi on Little Angel.
The elephant ate Little Angel's bed.
The horse got up on the wardrobe and licked
    all the paint off the wall.
Afterwards he made caca in the Camomile
    Tea.
"You see," said the elephant.

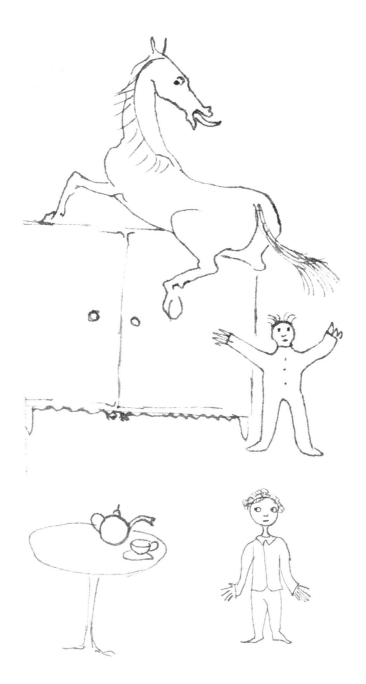

The Black Story of the White Woman

A white woman wore black.

Black with black.

She had black pyjamas and black soap.

All her things were black.

Black as night.

Black as coal.

But when the woman cried, her tears were
    blue and green like little parrots.

The woman cried a lot as she played the flute.

The
white
woman
dressed in
black
crying
and
playing
her flute.

The Gelatin and the Vulture

Ophelia made a big gelatin
For the party— It was a strawberry gelatin.
They knocked at the door—
It was the milk—
Ophelia liked the milkman—
They chatted—
Meanwhile
A vulture entered through
The kitchen window and
Saw the gelatin—he sipped a little
With his beak—
He liked it so much
That he took—more and more—
He felt so drunk
That he fainted—
He fell into the gelatin
As it solidified—
When Ophelia returned with the milk
She was horrified to see

A vulture
Solidified in her gelatin—
"Oh how horrible—what will my employers
    say."
At night when
The gelatin was served
The lady of the house was surprised
"What does it have inside?" She asked—
"It's a fruit" answered Ophelia—(little lies)
"I will eat it" said the master of the house
And he ate the vulture along with feathers
    and all—
"This fruit seems like a bird"
Said the master—

This is the Vulture's father—

And here is the Mother.

(Translated by Gabriel Weisz)

The Disgusting Story
of the Roses

Don Crecencio was a butcher

He also had a garden

But his flowers never grew

Because the Rabbits ate them all

—Even the Roses—

Don Crecencio was sad

Because he had no flowers

But was very fond of Rabbits—

What shall I do?

Then he prepared some roses

with ground Goat's Meat—

He smeared it over the roses

with lard—

"Now I have Roses"

Said Don Crecencio

Out came the ugly Flies

They played with the Goat's meat roses—
"It stinks"
Said the lady of the house—
Don Crecencio fetched his
    Scissors
And he cut all the flies'
    wings—
They were all running over
    the floor
Eating small Rabbit turds—
"Are they little turtles?" Asked the Child
"They are flies"

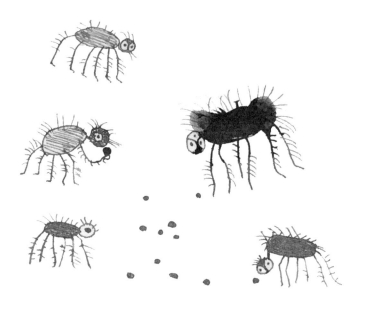

Answered Don Crecencio.

"They cannot play with the Roses"

The Badger came and ate all the Wingless

Flies—

Don Crecencio

Prepared more roses with Goat's meat

And with the others made chorizo

The garden smelled

Of goat.

(Translated by Gabriel Weisz)

45

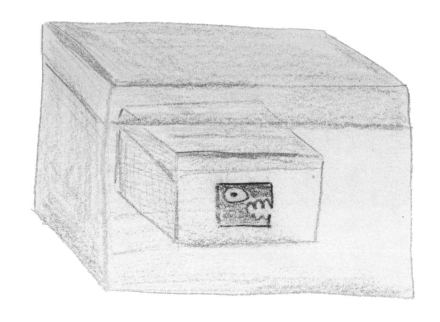

Here are
the three boxes:
the Green,
the Pink,
and the
little box
inside
that bites.

The frightening buffalo
and Señor Blue,

who shoots the buffalo.

The monster with the
black birthday cake.
It has three green candles.

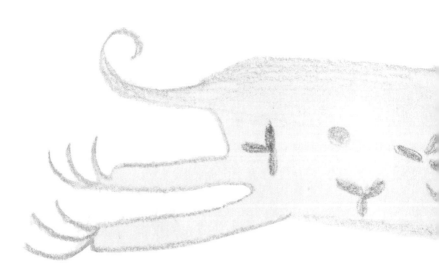

moustache

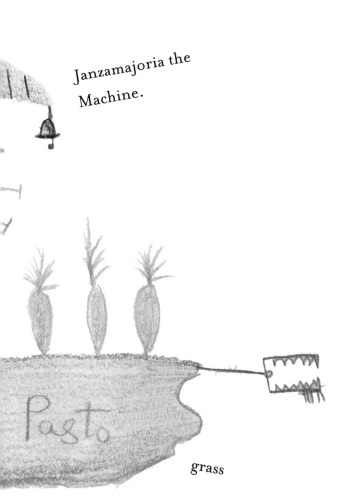

Janzamajoria the Machine.

Pasto

grass

The Lawyer's Son

Jeremy was the son of a Lawyer.

He liked making little holes in the sofa.

They looked like little mouths.

Jeremy put food into the little holes of the
sofa.

He gave them bread and butter, bacon,
spinach, and meat sandwiches.

The holes became more and more like
mouths. They grew teeth to chew the
food.

One day Jeremy forgot to give the little holes
their dinner.

One of them got cross and bit the Lawyer
when he sat down to read his newspaper.

"You'd better look out," said the Lawyer,
and he had all the little mouths sewn
up so that they could only say
"Mmmmmmmmmmm."

Jeremy made a very small hole under the sofa
and pushed up vitamins.

The sofa got very thin, but its legs grew.

Nobody can sit on it any more.

Only the madman with wings.

It can't be cleaned, it's too tall.

Leonora Carrington (1917–2011) was born in Lancashire, England, to an industrialist father and an Irish mother. She was raised on fantastical folk tales told to her by her Irish nanny at her family's estate, Crookhey Hall. Carrington would be expelled from two convent schools before enrolling in art school in Florence. She fled Europe during the Second World War and settled in Mexico, where she married the photographer Imre Weisz and had two sons. Carrington spent the rest of her life in Mexico City, moving in a circle of like-minded artists that included Remedios Varo and Alejandro Jodorowsky. Among Carrington's published works is a novel, *The Hearing Trumpet* (1976), and two collections of short stories. NYRB Classics publishes her memoir, *Down Below*, and her *Complete Stories* is published by Dorothy, a Publishing Project in the United States and by Silver Press in the United Kingdom.

SELECTED TITLES IN THE
NEW YORK REVIEW CHILDREN'S COLLECTION

ESTHER AVERILL
Jenny and the Cat Club
Jenny Goes to Sea
Jenny's Birthday Book
Jenny's Moonlight Adventure

PALMER BROWN
Cheerful
Something for Christmas

VICTORIA CHESS and
EDWARD GOREY
Fletcher and Zenobia

CARLO COLLODI and
FULVIO TESTA
Pinocchio

INGRI and EDGAR PARIN
D'AULAIRE
D'Aulaires' Book of Animals
D'Aulaires' Book of Norse Myths
D'Aulaires' Book of Trolls
Foxie: The Singing Dog
The Terrible Troll-Bird
Too Big
The Two Cars

ROGER DUVOISIN
Donkey-donkey
The House of Four Seasons

ELEANOR FARJEON
The Little Bookroom

LEON GARFIELD
Leon Garfield's Shakespeare Stories

RUMER GODDEN
Mouse House
The Mousewife

LUCRETIA P. HALE
The Peterkin Papers

RUSSELL and LILLIAN HOBAN
The Sorely Trying Day

RUSSELL HOBAN and
QUENTIN BLAKE
The Marzipan Pig

RUTH KRAUSS and
MARC SIMONT
The Backward Day

DOROTHY KUNHARDT
Junket Is Nice
Now Open the Box

MUNRO LEAF and
ROBERT LAWSON
Wee Gillis

RHODA LEVINE and
EVERETT AISON
Arthur

RHODA LEVINE and
EDWARD GOREY
*He Was There from the Day We
Moved In*
Three Ladies Beside the Sea

RHODA LEVINE and
KARLA KUSKIN
Harrison Loved His Umbrella

BETTY JEAN LIFTON and
EIKOH HOSOE
Taka-chan and I

ASTRID LINDGREN
Mio, My Son
Seacrow Island

NORMAN LINDSAY
The Magic Pudding

EUGENE OSTASHEVSKY
The Fire Horse: Children's Poems by
Daniil Kharms, Osip Mandelstam,
and Vladimir Mayakovsky

J. P. MARTIN
Uncle
Uncle Cleans Up

JOHN MASEFIELD
The Box of Delights

WILLIAM McCLEERY and
WARREN CHAPPELL
Wolf Story

JEAN MERRILL and
RONNI SOLBERT
The Elephant Who Liked to Smash
Small Cars
The Pushcart War

DANIEL PINKWATER
Lizard Music

OTFRIED PREUSSLER
The Little Water Sprite
The Little Witch
The Robber Hotzenplotz

VLADIMIR RADUNSKY and
CHRIS RASCHKA
Alphabetabum

CHRIS RASCHKA
The Doorman's Repose

ALASTAIR REID and BOB GILL
Supposing...

ALASTAIR REID and
BEN SHAHN
Ounce Dice Trice

BARBARA SLEIGH
Carbonel and Calidor
Carbonel: The King of the Cats
The Kingdom of Carbonel

E. C. SPYKMAN
Terrible, Horrible Edie

ANNA STAROBINETS
Catlantis

CATHERINE STORR
The Complete Polly and the Wolf

FRANK TASHLIN
The Bear That Wasn't

VAL TEAL AND
ROBERT LAWSON
The Little Woman Wanted Noise

ALVIN TRESSELT and
ROGER DUVOISIN
The Frog in the Well

ALISON UTTLEY
A Traveller in Time

T. H. WHITE
Mistress Masham's Repose

MARJORIE WINSLOW and
ERIK BLEGVAD
Mud Pies and Other Recipes